MANGO MADNESS MURDER

The Frosted Love Cozy Mystery Series, Book 15

SUMMER PRESCOTT

Copyright 2019 Summer Prescott Books

All Rights Reserved. No part of this publication nor any of the information herein may be quoted from, nor reproduced, in any form, including but not limited to: printing, scanning, photocopying, or any other printed, digital, or audio formats, without prior express written consent of the copyright holder.

**This book is a work of fiction. Any similarities to persons, living or dead, places of business, or situations past or present, is completely unintentional.

The Story Behind The Story

Finally! It took me fifteen books into the series before I could do it, but after this book I was finally able to take a look at my reviews without crawling into a corner and shuddering for a while. That's not to say that there weren't any critical reviews. There were. Definitely. But, I believed in this book so much because of what was happening in the character's lives, that I was able to look at the criticism, determine what was valid, and not have it crush my soul. There was some valid criticism, to be sure. I had done some things which screamed "new Cozy writer," and I was okay with that.

You see, it had started in the last book...the thing that gave me the confidence to withstand less than positive feedback. What was that magical thing, you ask? Love. I had gotten to really know and love my characters. I cried when I wrote the ending of the last book because I was right there in the moment with them and it moved me. This book had the same result, me in tears. Happy tears!

I believed in this story, even though, by some standards, maybe the mystery itself wasn't as strong as it could have been. My characters are living their lives and loving one another and spending some spare time sleuthing, and I was happy with that. One of the reviewers said that the series would make a better soap opera than Cozy Mystery series, and while I disagree, I reserve the right to take that as a compliment.

These characters are my friends, and I'm glad that they're becoming your friends too, dear readers. Thank you for sticking with Missy and the Cupcake Gang. You're family now. Y'all come back now.

Chapter 1

Melissa Gladstone, vivacious owner of *Missy's Frosted Love Cupcakes*, in LaChance, LA, and *Crème de la Cupcake* in nearby Dellville, sat across from her best friend, Echo, in her Dellville store, her hands wrapped around a mug of coffee.

"I can't believe that Mr. Wonderful finally proposed," Echo, the free-spirited former Californian remarked, popping a bite of a Morning Glory cupcake in her mouth. She owned the vegan ice cream shop across the street from *Crème de la Cupcake,* and often meandered over to catch up on the news of the day. She'd been in attendance at Missy's incredibly romantic surprise proposal and was ecstatic, and more than a tad envious.

"Believe me, I was more shocked than you were," Missy confessed, smiling and blushing a bit, remembering her normally reserved fiancé's grand gesture. "I'm still trying to process the whole thing."

"I thought you two weren't interested in a long-term relationship," the happy hippie teased, taking another huge bite of her cupcake.

"And yet, here we are, over a year later…" Missy laughed softly.

"Well, I'm sure there are quite a few people who go into something fully armed, emotionally, and determined to protect themselves, then find out that they're with someone safe," Echo observed, gazing at her friend fondly. "Personally, the last guy that I dated, turned out to be a serial killer," she made a face.

"Get a dog, they're more loyal anyhow," her friend winked.

"Says the girl who just got engaged," she shot back wryly.

"Before I ever met Chas, I had Toffee," Missy pointed out. Her love for her gentle golden retriever and spunky little maltipoo was well known, and Echo suspected that if it came down to a choice between the dogs and the fiancé, her friend would have to think long and hard about her choice.

"Hey, Ms. G.," Cheryl Radigan, the young manager of her Dellville store, called out from behind the counter.

Cheryl had married Ben, the manager of the LaChance store, after working with him for over a year, and now their baby girl, Cammie, who was Missy's goddaughter, was the center of their universe.

"What's up, honey?" Missy smiled at the lovely young woman.

"The mayor is on the phone for you," she replied, handing over the store's cordless handset.

"Oh! Okay, put him on hold for a second, I'll take it in my office," she instructed, pushing back her chair. "Sorry, duty calls," she said to Echo, giving her a hug.

"Let's just hope his daughter isn't engaged again,"

her friend laughed, referring to the mayor's spoiled little socialite. Several months ago, he'd convinced a more than reluctant Missy to plan his precious Priscilla's wedding, and it hadn't gone well, even before the groom-to-be was busted for art theft and murder.

"Fingers crossed," Missy nodded, disappearing through the swinging doors that led into the kitchen and heading for her cramped but spotless office.

"Mayor Chadwick," she answered with a smile, settling into her worn, but beautiful, "baseball glove" leather chair. "To what do I owe the pleasure?"

"Well, Melissa Gladstone, it's been quite some time since I've had the pleasure of speaking with you," the mayor responded. There was no such thing as getting straight to business in the South, there was always a preamble of socialization required.

Missy smiled. "Indeed, far too long," she agreed. "How's your family?" she asked the required question.

"Healthy and happy," the jolly man replied. "And I hear you have some exciting news of your own.

Congratulations! It's about time that detective of yours put a diamond on that pretty little finger."

"Yes, we're both very excited," Missy agreed, glad he couldn't see that she was blushing to the roots of her hair. The old-fashioned notion that a woman needed to be married in order to be fulfilled, stuck in her craw, but she understood that most of the folks that she knew felt differently. "So, what can I do for you today, Mr. Mayor?"

"Mr. Mayor, pish-posh, I told you darlin', call me Felton," he insisted with a chuckle.

"Yes, of course, Felton. How can I help you?" Missy corrected.

"Well, as I'm sure you're aware, we are in the heart of the mayoral election race here in LaChance," he began.

"Of course," Missy lied. The truth was, she generally ignored the yard signs, bumper stickers and patriotically-colored advertising that shouted out for each candidate during election season. Before voting, she would spend some time delving into issues that were most important to her and her businesses, and if she had any questions, she'd generally seek out the candidates and ask them personally.

"I'd like to see some of your work represented at the reception that takes place right after the mayoral debate, if that's possible. Maybe some cupcakes in red, white and blue?" he requested, as though he were already assuming the answer.

"I'm sure that we can make that happen, Felton, just have your secretary send me the specifics and I'll take care of it," Missy assured him, relieved that his request had been so simple.

"I want you to really outdo yourself on this one, little lady," he directed. "I'm hosting this shindig, and I want it to be remembered long after the debate is over."

"They'll be the best cupcakes that LaChance has ever tasted, I assure you," she smiled. After another round of pleasantries and promises to stay in touch, they hung up and Missy sighed. Projects done for the mayor were never as easy as they seemed, and she wondered what would be the catch this time.

Chapter 2

Missy rang the doorbell at Ben and Cheryl's comfy little blue and white cottage, looking forward to spending some time with the young family that she regarded as her own. They'd invited her to dinner, and her stomach growled in anticipation of Cheryl's homemade sour cream potato salad.

Cheryl answered the door with little Cammie balanced on her hip. "Hi! Come in, it's great to see you outside of the shop," she teased, giving her boss a big hug. Cammie reached her chubby little arms out and waggled her fingers, wanting her godmother to pick her up, and no second invitation was needed, Missy swooped her away from her mother gladly.

"Hey, little one," she kissed her favorite cherub on the nose.

"I'm so glad you're here," Cheryl called over her shoulder, heading into the kitchen. "Ben is on BBQ duty and I need to pull my biscuits out of the oven."

"It smells heavenly," Missy inhaled appreciatively.

Having grown up in the South, Cheryl's fresh baked biscuits were like fluffy, buttery clouds of perfection. There were various bowls and pans of food simmering, cooling and waiting to be attended to in the cozy little green and white kitchen, and Missy sat on a bar stool with Cammie after peering into the many containers.

"How can I help?" she asked as the young mother put biscuits on the cooling rack and took a short break to stir a crockpot of honey BBQ beans.

"Do exactly what you're doing," Cheryl instructed, turning off the oven and moving to the cutting board to chop dill for her amazing potato salad. "Having the little one entertained while I do nothing but cook is quite a treat," she grinned.

"Perfect," Missy cooed, looking into the warm chocolate eyes of the adorable child in her lap.

Ben came in, resplendent in his chef's apron, with a platter of fork-tender ribs. He'd basted them with just the right amount of his special homemade grilling sauce, and the aroma in the kitchen grew even more delicious.

"What should I do with this?" he asked, kissing his wife on the cheek.

"Just set them on the dining room table, it's a little bit too chilly to eat outside," she instructed, pointing her chef's knife in the direction of the dining room.

Ben set the platter on the table and came back to grab a heaping bowl of coleslaw and a pitcher of sweet tea, returning shortly, only to be handed a basket of fresh biscuits and the bowl of his wife's locally-famous potato salad. She ladled the beans into a serving dish and carried it to the table, beckoning Missy to follow her. After setting the beans on a pot holder, she took the baby from her boss and fastened the giggling child snugly into her high chair. The adults chattered gaily while helping themselves to the bounty before them, and Cammie tapped on her white plastic tray with a child-sized spoon.

"This is such a treat," Missy exclaimed, dabbing her biscuit in bean sauce. "My favorite foods and my favorite people, it doesn't get better than this," she smiled.

Ben and Cheryl exchanged a glance.

"Well, we actually had ulterior motives for inviting you over," Ben began, seeming as though he was trying to think carefully about what he wanted to say.

"Oh?" Missy put a forkful of potato salad in her mouth and set down her fork, blotting her lips with a napkin. "Is everything okay?" she frowned.

Cheryl smiled reassuringly. "No, we're fine…we just have some news, that's all," she looked pointedly at her husband.

Missy gasped. "You're getting a dog?" she asked, her face aglow.

The young couple laughed at her immediate assumption.

"No," Ben replied, smiling when her face fell in obvious disappointment. "Not that, at least not yet," he glanced fondly at his wife. "So...you know I'll be receiving my doctorate in May," he said, waiting for her nod. "Well, I've already received multiple job offers."

"Oh, Ben, congratulations, that's wonderful! I knew that would happen for you," she interrupted, gushing enthusiasm. She was as proud of him as if he was her own son, which for all practical purposes, he had been for the last few years.

"...and we've narrowed down the options and decided which one I'm going to take," he announced, letting his breath out in a rush.

"And?"

"And...I've been offered a position at UC Irvine. I'll be teaching a couple of classes and they're going to fund the research so that I can continue. It's the chance of a lifetime for a new post doc," he added.

"Oh Ben, that's wonderf...wait...did you say UC Irvine? As in California?" she asked, her eyes widening with realization.

Cheryl nodded, her eyes welling with tears.

Missy was stunned. She knew that Ben would be graduating soon, but the thought that they'd be leaving her hadn't quite sunk in yet. It wasn't so much that she'd be losing both of her store managers, but that she'd be losing her family. The thought of not seeing these incredible people every day, and not being there while Cammie was growing up, hurt her heart, but she knew that she should encourage the young family to spread their wings and fly.

"Congratulations, sweetheart, I'm so proud of you," she reached over and squeezed Ben's hand, tears running freely down her face.

"We know that our move is going to affect your shops, but we'll be able to help you with hiring and training," Ben assured her.

"Oh, Ben, I'm not worried about all of that. I'm just going to miss you all so much. I'm happy for you, but sad for me," she admitted wiping her tears and trying desperately not to smear her mascara. Cammie, sensing the change of mood in the room, stuck out her lower lip, and lowered her spoon, looking at the adults wide-eyed, with tears threatening.

"Oh, honey," Missy cooed, plucking her out of the high chair and crushing her to her chest. "It's okay, Nana's happy. It's okay, lovebug," she kissed the confused child's downy hair.

"I'm sorry to spring it on you like this," Cheryl said, wiping her own tears. "It's taken us a while to adjust to the idea too. I'm s-c-a-r-e-d to move away from Louisiana, I've never been further away than Florida, and that was only for my senior trip," she shrugged, looking young and helpless, but Missy knew better.

"You'll love it, I just know you will," she said as Cammie snuggled into her shoulder, sucking on two fingers. "You two are strong and smart and brave, and they'll be lucky to have you at UC Irvine," she promised, her own tears starting again.

Cheryl nodded and tried to smile, unable to speak past the lump in her throat. Ben reached for her hand.

"We'll definitely stay in touch," he said. "That little girl is going to grow up knowing who her Nana is," he nodded, getting a bit choked up himself.

As often happened to Missy in times of extreme emotion, she began to giggle. "Just look at the three of us," she shook her head. "You tell me some of the happiest news of your lives, and we sit here boohooing about it. We are going to stop this right now," she slapped her hand on the table with finality. "I'm going to call that wonderful fiancé of mine and tell him to pick me up from here after he gets out of work because I'm planning on being too tipsy to drive," she declared. "We're going to celebrate! Ben, you go grab us some wine," she ordered, and Ben got up immediately, grateful for being able to count on his effervescent boss to make lemonade out of whatever lemons life threw her way.

Chapter 3

"Okay, Grayson, we're going to need your artistic input for this project," Missy told her assistant at the Dellville store when she reviewed the meticulously detailed order for the mayoral debate. Tall, pale, dark-haired Grayson was an art student at the university, and one of the most creative individuals she'd ever met. All of the clients at the shop loved him, tattoos, piercings and all. The quiet, shy youth had captured the hearts of even the most skeptical and refined ladies in town, and had created some of the most beautiful and tasty cupcakes the shop had ever offered.

"No prob, Ms. G.," he replied easily, as usual. "What have we got?" he peered over her shoulder. Shaking her head at the mayor's particulars, she smiled and handed over the four-page order. "Wow," he said, taking it all in. "At least he knows what he wants, and it shouldn't be hard at all once I make some sketches for guidelines," the youth nodded. Missy could practically see his creative gears start spinning.

"Well then, my dear, get a plan together, run it by me, and we'll make sure we have the necessary ingredients," she patted him on the arm. "It's all yours," she said with a relieved smile, heading to the front of the shop.

Grayson was surprised. His boss usually allowed him a lot of creative freedom, but oversaw each plan herself. To allow him to come up with all of the ideas, and oversee the project himself, was a major step, particularly given the high-profile nature of this particular job. Grinning broadly, he dug into the mayor's specifics with gusto, images and applications building in his mind.

Missy went up front to see how Cheryl was coping, and saw that, although there were a handful of customers in the eating area, the young woman had things well in hand.

"Hey, I was just about to start restocking, want to help?" she asked brightly when her boss came out to check on her.

"Of course, just tell me what we need, and I'll grab the trays."

"Okay," Cheryl bent to peruse the display cases, pen and pad in hand. "Okay...we need...four Coconut Crème, six Carob Cappuccino, two Sinfully Strawberry, a dozen Mango Madness, and four Margarita Lime," she stood, peeling the top paper from the pad and handing it to Missy, who disappeared into the kitchen.

When she returned to the front, she saw Echo slouched over the counter by the cash register, talking to Cheryl and looking decidedly glum.

"Hey, girlfriend, long time no see," Missy greeted her, putting the tray of luscious cupcakes on top of the display case.

"Is that Carob Cappuccino?" her friend asked, sounding weary.

"Yes, it is," she replied handing one over. "You okay?"

"I will be, but it's gonna take two of these at least before I get there," she sighed.

Missy handed her another cupcake. "Go sit, I'll be there in a minute with fresh coffee," she ordered, giving Cheryl an apologetic look.

"I've got this," the young woman smiled with understanding. "I think Grayson just made a fresh pot of Costa Rican," she gestured toward the kitchen, letting her boss off the hook.

"Thank you," Missy mouthed silently, turned so that her distressed buddy couldn't see her.

"What's wrong, sugar plum?" she asked, upon returning with two piping hot mugs of java.

"I don't know exactly," Echo sighed. She took a gargantuan bite of her cupcake and chewed slowly, as though the very act of chewing was wearing her out. "I think I might be depressed," she shrugged her shoulders limply.

"Depressed? But, honey, why?" Missy brushed a stray lock of slightly frizzy, naturally fire-red hair back from her friend's brow.

"I don't know. I think part of it is that I've been really

homesick for California lately. I miss the beach, and the sunsets..." she trailed off and took a bracing swig of her coffee.

"Well there are pretty sunsets here in good ole Louisiana too," she was reminded lightly.

"Yeah, I know, but they're just not quite the same. Particularly when I don't have anyone to share them with," she looked down and swiped her forefinger across the top of her second cupcake, licking it clean.

"Sweetie, are you lonely? I'm so sorry, I've been a terrible friend," Missy moved her chair closer and hugged her. "We can spend a lot more time together, I'm going to be hiring several more people anyway, so I won't need to be here as much," she reassured her.

Echo smiled ruefully. "No offense, dearest, but you don't exactly have the right equipment to cure my loneliness," she raised her eyebrows meaningfully.

"Oh!" Missy exclaimed, her cheeks flushing crimson. "You mean...umm..."

"No, that's not what I mean," her friend sighed. "I just want a man who'll be nice to me – who'll take me to the movies, eat ice cream with me, give me a hug when I need one," she wished dreamily. "No offense, my beloved friend, but your arms are not nearly strong enough or hairy enough," she teased, finally cracking a genuine smile at having made her friend jump to a conclusion that made her blush.

"Oh, right, of course," Missy grinned, recovering.

"Not everyone has a Mr. Wonderful," Echo mused wryly.

"Well, I'll see if I can find you one," Missy promised, meaning it.

"What would I do without you?" was the fond reply.

Chapter 4

"Graysoooooon!" Missy's normally calm, cool, collected demeanor had temporarily taken leave as she prepared for the mayoral debate reception.

"Yeah, boss?" the youth came trotting over from where he had been putting finishing touches on a display.

Closing her eyes, taking a deep breath, and trying to remain calm, she said, "One of the star cupcakes for the flag has lost two of its points."

Her voice wavered just a bit, but Grayson was perceptive and knew that she was close to the end of her rope for some reason. Everything was going smoothly, but the young man knew that she was also consumed with wedding plans and finding replacements for Ben and Cheryl, so her stress level was completely understandable, if not entirely warranted.

"Ms. G.," he said, taking her by the shoulders and looking her dead in the eye, a bold move for the reclusive youth, "I've got this, okay? There are at least a dozen star replacement cupcakes in the van, I'll just grab one and bring it out to the display," he said, his confident manner calming her down significantly.

"Okay," she nodded, relieved. "I'm sorry. I don't know what's gotten into me today, I'm just feeling frazzled," she wrapped her arms around herself.

"You'll get through it, you always do," he replied, giving her a sweet smile before heading out to the delivery van.

Grayson had outdone himself this time, and Missy couldn't be more thrilled. The debate had gone well, despite the fact that the two men had, at times, looked like they were going to come to blows, and the reception was mere moments away from beginning. There was an American flag cupcake display, complete with the star-shaped cupcakes that had stressed her out, along with a cupcake replica of the town seal, and Grayson's piece de resistance, a life-sized cupcake cartoon rendering of the two candidates facing off with boxing gloves on, a masterpiece that filled several linen-covered tables, and was sure to be an instant hit.

When the last cupcake had been placed, it was merely minutes before the guests were scheduled to arrive.

"You did an amazing job, Grayson," Missy hugged him. "I'm so proud of you."

The young man grinned and blushed. "Thanks for letting me take charge of it, Ms. G., that really meant a lot to me," his head bobbed, and he thrust his hands into his pockets.

"That doesn't look a thing like my husband," a young woman's nasally voice droned nearby. Missy and Grayson turned at the comment to see who could've said such a thing.

"Excuse me?" Missy said to the well-groomed stranger in the yellow Jackie-O suit, trying to keep a lid on her temper. She could feel Grayson shifting from foot to foot beside her. Having grown up in a broken home, the young man couldn't stand conflict.

"Are you deaf? I said, that thing," she enunciated, jabbing a finger at the cupcake likeness of Mayor Felton Chadwick's rival. "Does not look at all like my husband, the Honorable Chester Kingsman," she snipped haughtily.

"I...uh...got the likeness directly from his campaign photo," Grayson mumbled, trying, in his non-confrontational way, to defend himself.

"Well then it clearly needed to be retouched," the woman sneered nastily.

"Now, wait just a minute," Missy stepped toward the rude critic.

"Oh, look," the candidate's coldly attractive and wickedly spoiled young wife had a wicked gleam in her eye. "You forgot his nostrils," she smiled sweetly and plunged two fingers into the cupcakes that formed Chester's nose.

Missy gasped as Grayson sprinted toward the staging

area. "You wretched human being!" she accused, horrified at the woman's behavior.

"You think I'm bad, wait 'til you meet my husband," she smirked, licking the frosting delicately from her manicured fingers.

Missy had to bite back her reply as the doors to the reception hall opened, admitting the two candidates, followed by the press and a large crowd of supporters on both sides of the aisle. Grayson charged back to the table, deftly slipping Missy the two new cupcakes that he'd fetched, removing the violated cakes and replacing them before the paparazzi reached the display.

"Thank you for saving the day, Grayson, I owe you," Missy said in a low voice as the candidates approached. "And as for that nasty woman, why I'd like to…"

"Hello, Mayor Chadwick, Judge Kingsman!" Grayson said loudly, cutting her off as cameras began snapping photos of the brilliant display.

"Thanks," she mouthed, before turning to smile at the two men who stood in front of her, admiring Grayson's work.

"Well, now, Melissa Gladstone, you've outdone yourself this time," Felton said, pumping her hand enthusiastically.

"Actually, all of this is the concept and artistry of this young man," Missy said proudly, introducing Grayson to folks that he considered to be local royalty.

"Young man," Chester Kingsman rasped, sounding out of breath. "You are indeed an artist – this looks exactly like me," he nodded with approval. Missy and Grayson exchanged a look, and both had to concentrate hard on not bursting into laughter.

"Thank you, sir," he replied, shaking the candidate's hand.

The two candidates stayed long enough to pose for some photos, publicly continue to debate some of their favorite topics, and sample a few of Missy's delightful goodies before retiring for the evening. The party continued for a couple of hours after their exit, with Missy and Grayson faithfully restocking cupcakes as needed.

"I am so ridiculously tired," Missy blinked, slumping

into a chair for a moment, prior to starting cleanup, after the last guest had been ushered out.

"Me, too," Grayson yawned and stretched. "But the sooner we clean up our stuff, the sooner we get out of here," he reasoned, heading to the van for boxes in which to place the leftover cupcakes. After major events like this one, Missy took the leftovers to the local homeless shelters for an evening snack.

Grayson came charging back into the reception hall moments later, white as a ghost.

"Goodness gracious, honey, what's wrong?" Missy's southern accent went into overdrive when she was scared.

The poor young man could barely get the words out. "Chester Kingsman is in the back of our van…and it looks like he's dead!"

Chapter 5

*P*olice swarmed the elegant reception hall and Missy and Grayson now had so much adrenaline racing through their veins that neither of them could even think about going to sleep, despite their earlier exhaustion. Detective Chas Beckett was overseeing the investigation and had interviewed all of the staff members who were still at the hall at the time before heading over to Missy and Grayson, who were huddled together at a small table.

"Did you look in the van?" Chas asked Missy quietly after sitting down across from the shaken pair.

She shook her head slowly. "I couldn't...I didn't want to see," was her numb reply.

"And you?" the detective asked Grayson.

The youth swallowed hard, remembering the gruesome sight and the coppery smell of blood. So much blood. "Yes, sir," he nodded, wide-eyed. "I saw."

"Was there anything that struck you as odd when you approached the van? Anything that seemed out of place?" he probed.

"I was a little bit surprised that it was unlocked, but then I just figured that I had probably done that by accident when I ran out here to fix Judge Kingsman's nose," he explained, receiving a startled look from Chas.

"His nose?"

Missy jumped in. "We had a strange encounter with Mrs. Kingsman right before the candidates came in, and she ended up ruining part of the display that featured her husband..." She went over the incident in detail for the detective, his brow furrowing deeper by the second. He rubbed his forehead in a telltale gesture that let Missy know that something was bothering him.

"What is it, Chas?" she asked, alarmed.

"The fact that you had an altercation with the candidate's wife shortly before his body was found in your van, rather complicates things," he made a face like he needed an antacid.

"But we didn't do anything," Grayson protested. "Judge Kingsman was actually really nice to us both and complimented the display that looked like him. Maybe the security cameras picked that up," he added hopefully.

"I'm sure the cameras picked up footage of the nastiness that happened with the Judge's wife as well," Chas sighed. "Well, you two can head on out, but the van is still being processed, and it's going to be a long night for me, so I'll have a patrolman take you home."

"Uh...actually, can he just take us to the shop? Both of our cars are there, and if my mom sees me get dropped off by a police car, there'll be heck to pay, especially if she's been drinking," Grayson requested, looking down at his shoes, his cheeks red.

Missy put a supportive hand on his shoulder, and the detective nodded.

"Of course," he said quietly. "Not a problem," he

assured the embarrassed youth, raising a hand to beckon to a uniformed officer.

The mood inside the police car was somber as they made their way back to *Missy's Frosted Love Cupcakes*. Missy had told Chas that the officers working the scene could snack on the leftover cupcakes that had been boxed up, and he simply nodded, not having the heart to tell her that they'd probably be collected and tested as potential evidence. When they were dropped off at the shop, the officer was kind enough to wait until they had hugged and were in their respective cars before pulling out of the back lot.

Chapter 6

*M*issy had done a lot of tossing and turning before finally dropping off into a fitful and nightmare-filled sleep in which she constantly seemed to be running away from someone...or something. Her phone buzzed insistently from its place on her night stand, taking a long time to penetrate her exhausted stupor.

"Hello?" she mumbled sleepily, trying to stifle a yawn.

"Well, well, well, Melissa Gladstone...looks like you've gotten yourself into quite the little pickle, now haven't you?" the mayor's voice sounded a bit sinister and was far too loud for the early hour at which he was calling.

Missy looked at her ancient radio alarm clock, saw that it was just after six and groaned inwardly. She always tried to be on her toes when dealing with Felton Chadwick, and after a sleepless night, she wasn't at all prepared to deal with him, particularly before she'd had her coffee – at least a pot of it.

"Umm...pickle? What?" she tried to physically shake the cobwebs from her brain by literally moving her head back and forth.

"I find it very interesting that the Honorable Chester Kingsman's body was found in your van," Felton drawled.

"Interesting? No, it's terrible...what an awful thing," Missy yawned again, wondering what the mayor was getting at.

"You know, little lady, scandals like this that can ruin a person," he said carefully.

"I'm sure you have nothing to worry about, Felton. Everyone knows that you're more than capable of beating your opponent fair and square. Clearly, you'd never resort to such horrible measures to win an election," she assured him, irritated that he had woken her up at such a ridiculous hour to talk about his reputation and campaign.

"You misunderstand me, Melissa..." he let the sentence hang for a moment, sounding like he was intentionally pausing for dramatic effect. "I'm not concerned about how this matter will affect me, my reputation is strong enough to weather almost any storm. My concern is how you're going to handle it when your businesses fail and your neighbors start locking their doors and windows because all the townsfolk know is that one of their very own government officials was found dead in your van," Felton finished, saying nothing more, letting it sink in.

"Felton Chadwick! How dare you insinuate that I had anything to do with this awful thing? You know me well enough by now to know that I couldn't possibly be a part of what happened. I planned your daughter's wedding for crying out loud!" Missy exclaimed, offended.

"Mmmhmm...and we all know how well that turned out," was the snide reply.

"It's not my fault that your precious Priscilla chose an art thief and a killer for her fiancé," she shot back.

"Here's what I know, young lady, and you listen good," the mayor ordered, and she could just picture the pompous smile on his face as he gave her a long-winded directive. "Someone is to blame for what happened. Now, because of the adversarial nature of our political system, silly, uninformed folks might start pointing their finger in my direction, which would be an utter travesty," Felton explained, as though talking to a child. "Because the body was found in your van, it seems to me that the shadow of doubt falls squarely on the shoulders of you and your dangerous-looking young assistant. I'm telling you this right now, Melissa Gladstone, if it comes down to a choice of either you or me taking the fall for this…most unfortunate occurrence, I guarantee you that I will be the last man standing, and you will fall. Am I making myself fairly clear?" he asked smugly.

"Did you do it?" Missy whispered, unable to help herself.

"I most certainly did not, and don't you forget it," Felton barked, his Southern accent heavy.

"I didn't either, and neither did Grayson," she said numbly.

"Don't bore me with details, Melissa. Good day to you now," he replied, hanging up with a quite cordial tone.

Chapter 7

Missy dragged herself out of bed, and went downstairs to start a pot of coffee, trying to work up enough strength to take Toffee, her gentle golden retriever, and Bitsy, her irrepressible maltipoo for a walk. She wanted to get to the Dellville shop early today, to check on Grayson, so after three cups of strong, black coffee, she took "the girls" out for a walk, then came back and showered, finally feeling somewhat human again after getting dressed and tossing her blonde curls up into a messy bun.

"G'mornin', Cheryl," the already-weary shop owner said, coming in the back door to the kitchen.

"Hey, Ms. G.," her manager replied, looking at her with concern. "How're you holding up?"

"I'm fine," she waved dismissively. "Where's Grayson?"

"I hope you don't mind, but after he told me what happened last night, I sent him home. He hadn't had any sleep and he looked just awful. I called Ben to ask if he could lend us Chris from *Missy's Frosted Love Cupcakes,* so he's on his way to cover Grayson's shift," she explained.

"You did the right thing, honey," Missy assured her. Chris was a friend of Ben's from grad school who had been hired right around the same time as Cheryl. He'd been involved with Echo's sister briefly, when she came out to visit from California, which had turned out to be a big mistake. The troubled young woman had him under her spell to the degree that she even managed to convince him to "temporarily borrow" some money from Missy's cash register. When an infuriated Missy found out what had happened, she considered firing the lad, but having seen Echo's sister in action, she decided to give him another chance, and had been nothing but happy with him ever since.

"I can't even imagine how that poor, sensitive young man must've felt, finding that body," she shuddered. "Can Chris stay all day?"

Cheryl shook her head. "No, he had been volunteering for Judge Kingsman's campaign, and they're having a meeting today to break the news to everyone. It's just so awful. Why would someone do such a thing?"

"I wish I knew, darlin', I wish I knew," Missy frowned.

"There was a policeman that came by here this morning, asking questions," she confided, wrapping her arms around her middle.

"About what?" Missy asked, alarmed.

"Grayson, mostly," Cheryl bit her lip, worried.

"Oh no..." Missy's heart sunk.

"Yeahhh..." her manager replied, crestfallen.

Their conversation was interrupted by Chris coming in the back door. Having showered, dressed and left for the day, without even a glance at television or social media, he had no idea what had happened, and was shocked when Missy told him of the previous night's events.

He shook his head in sad disbelief. "So that's why they're calling a meeting of the campaign staff," he sighed.

"I'm afraid so," Missy nodded.

"How's Grayson?" Chris asked, putting on his canvas apron.

"Not too well, I'm afraid," she replied, clearly worried about the young man.

"Well, with the way he looks and all, you gotta figure the cops would be taking a hard look at him first," he mused, tying a knot at the back of his waist and heading for the sink to wash his hands before stocking the cases.

Missy and Cheryl drew in a collective sharp breath.

"What an awful thing to say, Chris. We all know that Grayson wouldn't hurt a fly!" Cheryl came to the assistant's defense. "In fact, the other day, there was a spider in the eating area, and when I asked him to take care of it, he scooped it up in a cup and put it outside rather than squishing it like most people would've done."

"Hey, I live in the real world," he shrugged, undaunted. "When you choose to look like that, with long hair and piercings and tattoos, people look at you differently, that's all I'm saying. I'm not going to argue whether the stereotypes tend to be true or not, but that's just the way it is."

"Well, fortunately, those of us who know and love Grayson, won't be judging him by such ridiculous measures," Missy raised a disapproving eyebrow at Chris, who turned away quickly, heading for the unfrosted trays and the bowls of frosting.

"Hey, what's our Cupcake of the Day supposed to be?" he changed the subject, examining the unfrosted cakes that had been pulled out of the oven earlier.

"Mango Madness," Cheryl replied dully, unaware before this morning of just how appropriate having a Cupcake of the Day with "Madness" in the title would seem. "The frosting is in the bowl on the right, use the fluted tip," she directed, looking at

Chris thoughtfully, then exchanged a glance with her boss.

"Well, team, you guys can carry on here, I'm going to go see how Ben is managing, and maybe pop by Echo's store for a dish of Vanilla Bean Rice Dream," Missy said, reaching for her purse.

"I think that ice cream is entirely warranted under the circumstances," Cheryl agreed. "We'll be fine here, don't worry. If it gets really busy after Chris leaves, I'll call you," she promised.

Chapter 8

"How well do you actually know Grayson?" Chas asked Missy, his eyes locked on hers. They were having a quick dinner at their favorite crawfish café, before Missy went home to the girls and Chas spent another long night at the office, trying to solve the Kingsman murder.

"Quite well," she frowned at the fact that the detective would even ask such a thing. "Not only have I worked side by side with him for some time now, we've had some very in-depth conversations about important things," her tone was strident. She hated having the finger of blame pointed at Grayson. While it was true that he was the artist who created the rendering of Judge Kingsman that the man's wife had nearly destroyed, he certainly wasn't concerned enough about the incident to have then murdered the candidate. It made Missy wonder if the mayor hadn't been pulling strings behind the scenes to shift the focus away from himself and onto poor Grayson.

She sighed, dropping her head into her hands in frustration. "Look, Chas, I may be just a cupcake artist, but I really don't think that it takes a rocket scientist to figure out who the most obvious suspect should be. There's only one person in this town who would have the motive to kill Judge Kingsman, and that's his opponent, Felton Chadwick!" Missy insisted vehemently.

"Questioning my intelligence these days?" Chas raised his eyebrows with a slight smile.

"Oh, honey, you know I didn't mean it like that, but doesn't it make sense?" she persisted.

The detective took a deep breath. "When dealing with a public figure like Felton Chadwick, we have to be very careful, Missy. This man holds a lot of power in this parish, and we can't even consider making an accusation for a capital offense until we have far more than just a suspicion to go on," he said in a low voice.

"So, you think he did it too?" she asked, excited that he had seen her point.

"I didn't say that, but I will agree that he would probably be the most logical choice. People have killed for much lesser positions of authority," Chas admitted, carefully.

"What can we do to make sure that they stop being suspicious of Grayson?" Missy asked.

"Sweetie, there's nothing you can do. I have my best men on this, and we'll get it taken care of," he assured her. "Don't forget, when Grayson comes under scrutiny, you're not immune either," he warned.

"Why can't things just go back to being normal?" she asked plaintively.

"Why indeed," her fiancé agreed, kissing her hand.

They changed the subject at that point and made an effort to talk about anything other than the Kingsman murder – their upcoming wedding, Ben's graduation party, and hiring new managers for

Missy's business. It was refreshing to take a brief escape from reality, while munching on some good ole fashioned Southern comfort food, but their respite was abruptly cut short by the ringing of Missy's phone.

The caller ID showed that it was Samantha Lemmon, a member of the *Burgundies and Books* book club to which Missy belonged. She had gotten to know the young ER nurse better over the past few months and considered her to be a good friend, so despite the fact that she was enjoying Chas's company enormously, even under the current circumstances, she took the call.

"Hi, Sam," she said with a smile after pushing 'Accept' to take the call.

"Missy, oh my goodness, I'm so glad that you answered," Sam said in a hushed tone.

"Oh my, why? What's wrong, Sam?" Missy's heart began to pound within her chest, an overwhelming premonition of doom seeping into her soul.

"I'm not supposed to tell you this, okay, but I know that you would want to know…" her voice was nearly a whisper.

"What is it, Sam?" Missy interrupted, worried. "I won't tell anyone that you told me."

"An ambulance just came in a few minutes ago... Grayson was on it, and he didn't look good, Missy, I'm so sorry," the young nurse confided.

"What?" the color drained from Missy's face, and Chas reached for her hand, concerned. "Is he...?" she couldn't bring herself to ask the question.

"No, at least not the last time I checked. He's in surgery, I'll try to keep you posted, but I have to go now. I'm really sorry, but I have to go," she whispered. Dial tone.

Missy was shaken and stunned. Chas had seen her reaction and signaled for the check, so he was able to spirit her from the restaurant before the storm of tears that threatened swept her away. She told him what the phone call had been about, lamenting that, since she wasn't actually related to Grayson, she wouldn't have access to any information about him.

"You won't, sweetie, but I will," the detective assured her, his jaw set.

"I don't even know what happened to him," Missy murmured, tears flowing freely.

"I'm going to drop you off at home, then I'm going to find out," he promised. "As soon as I know something, I'll call you."

Chapter 9

Chas Beckett strode into the Emergency Room on a mission. He too had grown to know Grayson a bit over the last year, and was concerned about the young man whom his fiancée loved like a son. Spotting an officer hovering near the intake desk, he made a beeline to him to find out what had happened.

"Were you at the scene for the last ambulance that came in?" he asked the cop, one of his own guys that he knew well.

"Yeah, we got there before the EMT's, it was pretty messy," he said, lifting up his pant leg slightly to show the blood spatters on his shoe.

"What happened?" Chas inquired casually, sounding much calmer than he felt at the moment.

"Assault with Intent is what we're probably looking at. The kid was so beat up that he could hardly talk, broken bones, internal injuries, you name it. The only thing he kept saying that we could even understand was "red pickup truck," the officer filled him in.

"Is he going to make it?"

"Tough to say. Hope so," the officer shrugged and shook his head.

"Suspects?"

"Not yet, we sent a few units to comb the area for a red pickup truck, but nothing turned up."

"Where did the attack take place?"

"In the little alley behind the cupcake shop over on Main. Kid was in a sleeping bag by the back door. There was a woman walking her dog who found him and called us," the officer explained.

"Did she see anything?" Chas frowned, wondering why Grayson had been sleeping behind the shop.

"Nahhh...nothing but a bloody kid, clutching his sleeping bag. She stayed with him until we got there, then left after we took her statement."

"Has the next of kin been contacted yet?"

The officer puffed out his cheeks and blew out his breath slowly. "Yeah, and boy is that one a winner. We found the kid's mama after running his ID, and when we called her up, she ranted and raved about how much trouble he was and how she had thrown him out because she didn't need bad influences in her house – she sounded drunk as a skunk, but when we told her that her bad seed was in the hospital fighting for his life, suddenly she's Mother of the Year and needs a ride to the hospital. What a piece of work," he shook his head. "I sent a unit to go pick her up and bring her here, there's no way in the world I'd let her behind the wheel of a car the way that she was slurring."

"Any idea how long he'll be in surgery?" Chas asked, looking at his watch.

"Nope, I'm just waiting here to see if we need to find a raging bully or an actual killer. Looks like it could go either way," the cop replied.

"Understood," the detective nodded. He was about to say something else, but before he could open his mouth to speak, a woman who could only have been Grayson Myers' mother came bursting into the waiting room.

"My baby, my baby," she brayed, oozing tears and snot and reeking of cheap beer.

Petaluma Myers had to have been pushing fifty, and wore faded denim cut-off jeans, a t-shirt featuring an ad for a heavy metal concert in the late nineties, and filthy bubble-gum-pink shower shoes. Seeing the police officer standing with Chas, she lurched her way over to them, entirely unable to walk in a straight line, and flipping her bleached blonde hair with black and grey roots coquettishly over one bony shoulder, she appraised both men, but addressed herself to the uniformed one.

Wiping her nose with the hem of her shirt, and "accidentally" baring more than her share of midriff, she gazed pathetically at the officer.

"Where's ma son? I wanna to see ma baby," she sniffed, staggering sideways so profoundly that both

Chas and the uniformed cop reached out to steady her.

"Your son is in the operating room, ma'am, the doctors will come out to talk to you when they're done," the officer told her, the tang of chronic alcohol intake that emanated from her stinging his nostrils.

"Wha did he do?" she slurred. "Was it his fault? Cuz, I'll kick his…"

"No, it wasn't his fault," the cop interjected, before Grayson's mother said something that might end up landing her in jail.

"Oh, good," she nodded unsteadily, looking at the floor. "I doan feel so good…" she muttered, looking a little green.

"I'm going to leave you with this," Chas looked at his colleague apologetically and headed for the door. "Keep me posted." He heard the unmistakable sound of retching and a liquid splat on the sterile hospital floor as the doors whooshed shut behind him. He sympathized with the officer, and made a mental note to buy the guy a steak sometime soon.

"So, how is he?" Missy demanded, burying her face in Chas's chest when the detective came over after leaving the hospital. "What happened? Is he going to be okay? Was there an accident?" she continued to ask, terrified of the worst.

Her fiancé wrapped his arms around her and kissed the top of her head, waiting for her to stop asking questions so that he could try to answer a few of them. She realized what she was doing and pulled back a bit, taking Chas's hand and pulling him over to the couch, where she had wine waiting.

"He's still alive at this point, but I don't know what his prognosis looks like. He was in surgery while I was there, and I left word that I want to be notified with updates on his condition," the detective explained gently, pouring his distraught fiancée a glass of Merlot. He handed her the glass and continued.

"He was assaulted, profoundly so, and suffered broken bones and internal injuries, but I don't know the extent of them."

Tears streaked down Missy's cheeks and she took a swig of her wine, trying to absorb the information without breaking down entirely.

"Do they know who did it? Did he say anything?"

"He was pretty incoherent, from what I understand. The only intelligible thing that they could make out was that he kept repeating "red pickup truck." Chas took a small sip of his own wine, thinking that he might have to investigate the murder of Grayson Myers tonight if the poor kid didn't make it through surgery.

"There's no way to tell who did this to him, but I would guess that it's someone who was trying to send a very clear message," the detective said grimly.

"What kind of message?" Missy asked wide-eyed.

"Either it was a bunch of Judge Kingsman's supporters who were furious and looking for revenge, or, more likely, Mayor Chadwick whispered in the ears of a few thugs and made a few suggestions," Chas's jaw muscles flexed.

"Do you think he would do that?" Missy was horrified.

"He's a very powerful man, who will do whatever he needs to do to stay on top," the detective set down his wine glass. "I'd bet my last dollar that he'll be giving a press conference in the morning and saying something about how the fine citizens of LaChance saw the opportunity to exact justice for the murder of an innocent and followed through on it," he predicted, disgusted.

Chapter 10

Missy switched off the television, utterly disgusted. Chas was right, she had just been watching the mayor's press conference regarding the "tragic retaliation," that had been visited upon a "person of interest" in the Kingsman murder case. The conniving man even had the audacity to say that, "While I completely understood the impulse to impart justice, I cannot condone for an instant the concept of citizens taking the law into their own hands." He further cautioned other would-be vigilantes to refrain from further action in order to give "our fine law enforcement professionals," the opportunity to do their jobs. He sounded rational, magnanimous and entirely false in Missy's opinion, and she had half a mind to march right down to his office and call him out on it.

Chas prudently pointed out that it was far more important for her to focus on staying as far away from Felton Chadwick as possible until the murder was solved once and for all. He honestly hoped that she didn't position herself as his next target for speculation. Grayson was still in the ICU, and Detective Beckett felt that if the youth ended up dying, the mayor would most likely pull as many strings as he had to in order to have Grayson declared the murderer and subsequently have the case closed, with no one the wiser. If the young man pulled through, however, the mayor might either go after him again, or might target Missy, which was why Chas needed to solve the case while Grayson was alive and, for the moment at least, safely tucked away in the hospital. An armed guard had been posted and would remain outside his hospital room for the duration of his stay, or until the crime was solved.

Missy was upset that she couldn't go visit Grayson in the ICU. She understood why, but if only she could see his face, even if it was mangled and broken, at least she could see the rhythm of his breathing and know that, at this moment in time, he was alive. Samantha Lemmon had been keeping her informed as to his condition, as well as regaling her with tales of Petaluma Myers' interactions with doctors, the nursing staff and the security guards. Apparently, no one had yet seen Grayson's mother sober, and her tendency to regurgitate her most recent libations was legendary. According to Sam, the nurses on Grayson's floor drew straws to see who had to deal with her when she either passed out or vomited.

"Can't they just put her in a treatment program?" Missy asked, frustrated on Grayson's behalf.

"Not unless she commits a crime or checks herself in willingly, and believe me, we've tried. It's not going to happen," Sam said sadly.

Missy felt like she was caught up in a hellish limbo. The mayor made his speeches, Grayson held on to life by a thread, and thus far, no progress, as far as she could tell, had been made on the investigation. She needed a break, she needed to step away from the drama in her life and breath, she needed ice cream with Echo. Driving over to Dellville, her spirits lifted a bit at the thought of quality time with her best friend. Her heart dropped to her knees however, when she pulled into the parking lot of Sweet Love, the vegan ice cream shop. Surely there must be some mistake…there was a For Sale sign stuck in the patch of grass out front.

In such a hurry that she forgot to even lock her car, Missy dashed into the little shop, terrified that the sign might have been placed there intentionally.

"Hey, girlfriend!" Echo smiled when Missy came blazing into the shop, wild-eyed and breathing hard.

"Echo, did you know that there's a For Sale sign in front of the shop?" she asked, ignoring her friend's greeting.

"Of course I know, silly, I put it there," she replied, then, seeing Missy's face, she picked up a clean ice cream scoop. "You need Vanilla Bean," she prescribed, knowing that this wasn't going to be a fun conversation. She came out from behind the counter, bowl in hand and gave her stunned bestie a big hug. "Come, sit," she directed, walking over to a table, trying to entice Missy to move with a bowl of her favorite treat. The traumatized woman sat numbly across from her friend, too shocked to utter a sound.

"Remember when I told you I was homesick for California?" Echo asked, receiving a slow nod for an answer. "Well, I decided that, as much as I try, I can't forget my home. Louisiana is wonderful and beautiful, and the people are all so sweet and I love you to death, but California is home, so I'm moving back," she explained gently, pushing Missy's bowl of ice cream closer to her. The sad and stressed out woman looked mutely down at the rapidly melting treat and burst into tears.

"Why is everything going wrong?" she cried, all the stress and tension that she'd been carrying breaking free in a flood of emotion. "Grayson might die, and if he doesn't die, he might go to jail, and if he doesn't go to jail, I might, even though it's all the mayor's fault, and Ben and Cheryl are moving away and taking my goddaughter with them, and now you're moving away and my whole life is just falling apart," she wailed, putting her head in her hands and sobbing.

"Missy, hey…" Echo hurt for her dear friend. "I'm not going away forever, I'll come back to visit, and I'll definitely still be your Maid of Honor when you marry Mr. Wonderful," she came to stand by her heartbroken friend, then knelt by her chair, stroking her back while she cried.

"What am I going to do without you? How on earth am I going to cope with my crazy life?" she murmured, her breathing punctuated by hiccups from her tears.

"Well, we can Skype a lot, and I promise I'll come visit too. You know we can't stay apart for any length of time," Echo grinned fondly, grabbing her friend and wrapping her in a warm hug. "I love you, girl. That's never going to change."

"Promise?" Missy asked weakly.

"Promise."

Chapter 11

Missy had been working off her angst by baking non-stop, and had just turned off the mixer in the kitchen at the LaChance shop, when she heard Ben call out, "Ms. G.!" from the front. Hearing the distress in her manager's voice, Missy sprinted to the front of the store, narrowly missed by an object that went flying by her head.

She saw Ben behind the counter, covered in cupcake and frosting, holding a tray up like a warrior's shield, and was startled when a Purple People Pleaser cupcake splatted against the side of her head. Her gaze found the source of the barrage, a very angry Mrs. Kingsman. She had positioned herself next to all of the top-of-the-counter covered glass plates and was firing fresh cupcakes at Ben, Missy, and anything in her path as hard as she could.

"Mrs. Kingsman!" Missy scolded. "Stop it right now," she ducked as a series of three cupcakes in a row headed her way. "I know you must be upset, but this is not how adults handle these things," she popped up to say, then ducked again as Celia Kingsman reloaded.

"Your dreadful little punk-rocker employee killed my Chester," she screamed, red-faced.

"No, he didn't Mrs. Kingsman, I promise you that," Missy stuck her head up for a bit too long and got thwacked right in the forehead with an Apple Caramel Crisp cupcake, the sticky topping gluing her curls to her face. Brushing aside the mess, she tried again. "This isn't going to solve anything, please stop," she pleaded, really not wanting to have to call the police.

"I'm not going to stop until I feel better, and that could take a while," Celia shrieked. "Chester may have been a fat, pompous, jerk, but he was all I had," she seemed to deflate, still holding two cupcakes in each hand.

"I know, and I'm really, terribly sorry for your loss, but it had nothing to do with Grayson or my store, so why don't you just put those cupcakes down and go home and we'll forget this ever happened, okay?" Missy spoke softly, trying to calm the agitated widow.

"Never," she raged, plowing Missy squarely in the face with a Margarita Madness cupcake.

Just then, as Missy stood there, too stunned to move, wiping frosting out of her eyes and hair, the bell over the door jangled, distracting Mrs. Kingsman from her task as Chas walked in. Quick to assess the situation, he walked right up to the widow, his hands held out in a conciliatory manner.

"Okay, now, let's all just calm down," he said, in a slow, soothing voice.

"Everyone needs to stop telling me to calm down," Celia Kingsman screeched. "You calm down!" she hissed between her teeth, crushing the remaining cupcakes in her hands into the front of the detective's Savile Row suit. Even before inheriting a third of his late father's fortune, Chas had always dressed well. This one would make his dry cleaner really wonder. "Take that!" she said as her parting shot and stormed from the shop. Missy and Ben came out from behind the counter and the three cupcake-covered friends observed Celia get into her silver European car and drive away. Ben and Missy looked first at each other, then at Chas, and burst into laughter.

"Oh, gosh, look at this mess," Missy surveyed the damage when the gales of laughter had passed. Chas, none too amused, had gone to the employee bathroom to see if he could salvage his shirt and suit coat, his tie was clearly a total loss.

"I'll get some trash bags and cleaning supplies," Ben said, heading toward the back and nearly mowing over Chris, who was coming in to start his shift.

"Whoa, did you guys have a food fight?" he chuckled, glancing at the mess on the walls, the floor, and the people in the shop.

"It's a long story," Missy sighed. "Will you please go grab the push broom and start on the floors?"

"No problem," Chris grinned, still confused. When

he turned, he nearly collided with a slightly damp Chas.

"Hey, Detective, how ya doin'?" he asked cordially, extending his hand for Chas to shake.

"A bit better now that I no longer have Margarita Madness squished into my suit jacket," he replied dryly, giving Chris a strange look.

"I don't even want to know," the young man laughed, heading for the kitchen.

"Hey, beautiful," the handsome detective called out to his fiancée, walking over to her. She stood, wiping sticky hands on the front of her apron. "You look delicious, but something just came up and I need to get to work. Dinner later?" he asked. She nodded and kissed him, passing along a smear of vanilla buttercream frosting that had been on her lips. "Yup, delicious," he nodded, heading for the kitchen.

"Where are you going?" she asked, puzzled because he had come in the front door.

"Just want to check out the scene of Grayson's attack one more time," he explained easily. That struck

Missy as a bit odd, but she was entirely too busy at the moment to dwell on it.

She had heard earlier in the day that Grayson had finally moved from the ICU and was now recovering in a regular room, but still had an armed guard around the clock, just in case. She had planned to go see him right after work today, but now she'd have to go home and shower first. With Chris and Ben's help, she had the mess cleaned up in short order, but decided to close for the day anyway, since she and Ben were such sweet, sticky messes. Her sensitive skin was beginning to get irritated, and she knew that if she didn't get home and shower soon, she'd develop hives.

"We don't have to close. I can handle the afternoon traffic," Chris offered.

"Are you sure?" Missy asked, thinking it over. Chris had closed for her on more than one occasion since his mistake with Echo's sister, and had been perfectly fine, so she knew she could trust him.

"Of course," he replied. "There've been quite a few times when Ben has left me alone during the slow time in the afternoon, it's a piece of cake...no pun intended," he joked. "But seriously, I'll be fine, you two can go do what you need to do," he assured her.

"Thanks so much, Chris, you're a lifesaver! I can't tell you how much I've appreciated you stepping up and contributing at both stores while Grayson recovers, it means a lot to me," she smiled at the young man, making him blush.

"Don't worry about it, I've got this," he said, turning his attention to the push broom.

Chapter 12

Missy had been incredibly relieved when she had visited Grayson. He looked battered, bruised and torn, but was clearly alive, despite not being able to smile because of the stitches in his face. She had stayed with him until visiting hours ended, stroking his hair back from his forehead and lightly resting her hand on his one intact arm because his hands were a mess of cuts, bruises and broken bones. Petaluma alternated between snoring loudly in the chair in the corner and casting hateful glances at Missy behind her back. Grayson didn't want his mother to be in the hospital with him, but the one time that he'd tried to communicate that fact, she'd thrown such a hysterical fit that he decided to just silently endure her presence. When Missy left the hospital, he'd been sleeping, and she fervently hoped that the troubled woman who had birthed him wouldn't disturb him.

"How was he?" Chas asked, over fettuccini at their favorite Italian restaurant.

"As good as can be expected, I suppose. He was still pretty out of it on pain meds, and he couldn't smile because of his stitches, but it seemed like he was glad to see me," Missy replied, sad to see Grayson suffering, but ever so grateful that he had survived and would be back to normal at some point. Thankfully, his left hand was merely cut and bruised, not broken, so his artistic endeavors shouldn't be impacted, which was very good news indeed.

"I have to warn you, I'm waiting on a phone call, regarding some lab results, and once it comes in, I'll most likely have to go and arrest someone," Chas said mysteriously, twirling pasta around his fork.

"The mayor?" Missy leaned forward and whispered.

"No, actually...it's..." he stopped abruptly as his phone rang. He glanced at the screen quickly. "This is the call I've been waiting for."

"Detective Beckett," he answered. "Yes. And was it? Conclusively? Get me the warrant, and meet me at his home address, I'm headed out now." Chas hit End and stood to go. "I prepaid for dinner because I knew that this might happen. My apologies beautiful, do you mind taking a cab?"

"Not at all, but Chas...who are you arresting?"

"I'll stop by your place tonight after he's booked and tell you all about it," the dashing detective promised, kissing his future bride.

"Chris??" Missy was astounded. "Chris was the killer? But...how? Why? And how on earth did you figure that out?" she demanded. "All this time, I thought it was the mayor!" She had pounced on the detective, peppering him with questions the moment that he'd walked in her door. Dressed hastily in the first set of yoga pants and t-shirt that she could find after jumping out of bed that morning, she poured them both coffee and sat expectantly at the breakfast bar in her kitchen.

Chas shook his head. "The mayor is much smarter

than that. He might lie, cheat, bribe or torture to hang on to his power, but he wouldn't kill someone, or on the off chance that he had to, he'd never do his own dirty work," he explained. "That day that I walked in, when Celia Kingsman was pelting you and Ben with cupcakes, I went to the rest room afterward to clean some of the frosting out of my suit coat..." he began.

"Oh, right! Did it come out?" Missy interrupted.

"Yes, my dry cleaner is a wizard," he said absently, returning quickly to the topic of importance. "...and when I came out of the bathroom, Chris nearly ran me over."

"Okay..." Missy said, listening intently.

"He held his hand out to me to shake it, and I noticed that it was pretty significantly bruised, with lots of little nicks and cuts – the kind of nicks and cuts that come from hard impact against things like teeth," Chas said grimly. Missy gasped, putting her hands over her mouth.

"So...on a hunch, I decided to go out the back door, and sure enough, there was a red pickup truck. I ran the plates and confirmed that it belonged to Chris. His fingerprints were on file from when he stole from you last year, so I had the lab run them against the prints in the back of the van, on Chester Kingsman's cuff links and on the murder weapon and they were an exact match."

"Ugh," Missy said, chilled to the bone at the thought that a trusted employee, whom she'd been gracious to and had given a second chance, not only betrayed her, but was a murderer. "I probably don't want to know, but...what was the murder weapon?" she grimaced.

"An ice pick, that's why we suspected Grayson. It was nearly identical to the one that your team uses to chip ice from the inside of your freezers, but when we tried to match it against the one that was still in your shop, where it was supposed to be, it was from a different manufacturer, and it had Chris's prints all over it," the detective explained.

"But Chris had his entire future ahead of him, and he was a Criminal Justice grad student – he should've known that he wouldn't get away with that!" she exclaimed, puzzled.

"From what he said once we'd handcuffed him, he thought his knowledge of Criminal Justice would help him get away with it. He complained about the quality of his education," Chas shook his head in disbelief.

"He confessed?" Missy was astonished.

"I think he was so disgusted with himself for having been given a second chance and throwing it away, that he just wanted to 'fess up'," her fiancé shrugged.

"But why did he do it in the first place?" she asked, baffled.

"Well, that's an entirely different facet of the story. Chris had apparently been romancing Celia Kingsman for quite some time – that's why he volunteered to work on his campaign, because he'd get to see her more often, and there'd be more opportunities to slip away together without anyone thinking a thing about it," the detective raised his eyebrows at the scandal. "He had overheard you and Grayson talking about the debate event and figured it was the perfect opportunity to eliminate Judge Kingsman and frame Grayson for it."

"Grayson wouldn't hurt a fly, and everyone knows it. Why would Chris try to frame him?" Missy frowned at the unfairness of it all.

"It seems that in his world, people who look and behave differently, make easy targets. Personally, I think he was intimidated by Grayson's refusal to conform," Chas guessed.

"Was Celia in on it with Chris?"

"Celia had no idea that Chris killed her husband. Like everyone else, she thought that Grayson had done it, or perhaps the mayor, but that was a long shot in her mind. So, apparently, last night, after you left Chris to close up the shop, he emptied the cash register and fled to the Kingsman mansion, hoping to get Celia to run away with him. When she found out that, not only was he just a poor grad student, but that he was the villain who had killed her meal ticket as well, she pushed a secret button on her nightstand to call her private security guards, and by the time we got there with a warrant for his arrest, they already had him cuffed.

"Wow," Missy was amazed. "He stole from me again?

I guess I'm just a really bad judge of character," she shook her head sadly.

"Oh, I don't know," he teased, moving in for a kiss. "You chose me."

Chapter 13

"I may have a buyer," Echo said excitedly as she sat down across from Missy in their favorite corner of *Crème de la Cupcake*.

Missy put down her coffee cup. "Don't sound so happy about that, I'm still trying to come to terms with the fact that I won't be seeing you every day," she said ruefully.

"I'll be here for all of the important stuff," the California girl reminded her best friend.

"I know," Missy said glumly. "I'm trying to be happy for you, but I just want to selfishly keep you here," she admitted.

"I know, honey, I'm going to miss you too," Echo said softly. They blinked rapidly, then both looked down, took a bite of their cupcakes and washed it down with coffee, having a moment.

"So, on a happier note, how are things going with the wedding planning?"

It seemed as though anytime Missy even heard the word wedding these days, it struck a chord of fear in her heart.

"Logistically, everything is in place," she said carefully, avoiding her friend's eyes.

"And what's bothering you?" Echo probed, tilting her head, compelling Missy to look at her.

"It's just...this is huge, Echo," she murmured, overwhelmed. "I mean, this isn't just "should we do pizza or Cajun tonight?" – it's spending the whole rest of our lives together, you know?" her eyes were wide.

"You love him, right?"

Missy blushed. "Of course I do."

"And he loves you...?"

"He says he does," she made a face.

"Have you known him to be a liar?" Echo looked at her pointedly.

"No, of course not, but...he's so..."

"Oh, trust me, honey, I know. He's handsome, intelligent, classy, wealthy, and the sweetest guy ever, right?"

"Exactly!" Missy exclaimed. "What on earth would someone like that want with me?" she worried.

Echo shook her head with a smile. "Well, first, I think anyone who has ever been in love has felt that way about their significant other, and, second, you're pretty darn terrific yourself, girlfriend."

"Of course *you* would think so, you're my best friend," she pointed out. "I would hope that makes you naturally biased."

"True, but Chas is your best friend too," she reminded her. "That man sees you for all the good and wonderful things that make you who you are, just like I do. Think about it – you took over your parent's business at seventeen after they died, you put yourself through school while running a successful business, you volunteer in the community, you've created a family out of your staff, and you have the best gal pal in the whole world," she teased. "What's not to like? Did you ever stop to think that, by not feeling like you're good enough for him, you're questioning his taste and intelligence? Does he seem to be a man who's lacking in either of those qualities?" she demanded, practically.

Missy was silent for a moment. "Hmm...I never thought about it that way," she nodded.

"You have a classic case of cold feet, my dear, so put on your figurative bunny slippers and get over it," Echo advised, patting her hand. "He loves you, you love him, you're getting married in two weeks, end of story."

Two weeks. In two weeks, Missy would become Mrs. Gladstone-Beckett. She giggled when she thought of her new name, it reminded her of a medieval princess, but she had to admit that she loved the thought of adding Chas's name to her own. She loved him with all of her heart, and Echo was right, she just had to get past her jitters and sally forth.

Ben and Cheryl had smiled secret smiles, indulging their boss' need to be in perpetual motion to work through her stress over the past few weeks. She'd breeze into her shops, bake like a madwoman, then disappear to make wedding arrangements, leaving them shaking their heads in amusement.

Missy was standing in the kitchen, creating a new Cupcake of the Day flavor, a Chocolate Cheesecake Dream that was sure to be a hit. She made dense, moist, dark chocolate cupcakes, filled them with vanilla bean cheesecake cream and topped them with dark chocolate mousse frosting, drizzled with a red raspberry reduction. Seeing Cheryl enter the kitchen, she put down the spoon with which she had just applied the finest drizzle of raspberry and held one up excitedly.

"You have to try this!" she exclaimed holding the sublime example of cupcake art out to her manager. "It may very well be the best one yet."

Cheryl grinned at Missy's bright-eyed enthusiasm and took the cupcake. "You have a visitor out front," she said, wiping a smudge of flour from her boss' cheek.

"Oh?" Missy said, reflexively wiping her hands on a kitchen towel. Cheryl's mouth was too full of cupcake for her to elaborate, so she told her that she'd just go see who it was.

Missy's sunshine smile faded when she saw who waited for her on the other side of the counter.

"Mayor Chadwick," she greeted the rotund man in the pinstriped suit tonelessly.

"Good morning Melissa Gladstone," he greeted her as cheerfully as ever, choosing to ignore her return to addressing him formally, rather than by his first name. "I came down here today, little lady, to apologize for my improper assumption that you or your young helper had something to do with the tragic and untimely death of my opponent," Felton spread his hands magnanimously, and Missy wondered how it was that he made even an apology sound like some sort of campaign speech.

"It's fortunate that the real killer was found and is in custody," Missy replied coolly, not letting him off the hook by gratefully accepting his well-staged apology.

"Indeed. That detective of yours is a fine example of a law enforcement professional," the mayor nodded. "So, now that we have all of that nastiness behind us…" he began, rubbing his hands together.

Of course. The mayor hadn't actually come in to apologize to her, he'd come in because he needed something and figured that she wouldn't have given him the time of day without an apology. That would be a correct assumption on his part.

"What do you need, Mr. Mayor?" she sighed, cutting to the chase.

"I have an event coming up in three weeks that I…"

"Let me stop you right there," Missy held up a hand, startling the official who certainly was not accustomed to being interrupted. "Chas and I are getting married in two weeks, and will be on our honeymoon after that. If you have an event in three weeks, you'll have to discuss the details with my manager, Ben, and he'll let you know whether we're booked already or whether he can take your project on," she directed.

"Married? Well now, congratulations are in order!"

he exclaimed. "I don't believe my invitation has arrived as yet," he looked at her pointedly.

"Really?" she raised an eyebrow at him. "Imagine that."

Chapter 14

Missy's eyes were large as she gazed at her reflection in the mirror while Cheryl and Echo fussed with her veil. This was really happening, she was really getting married.

"I'm freaking out right now," she announced, too nervous to be anything but blatantly honest. The flurry of fluffing stopped, and Echo knelt down on one side of her, Cheryl on the other.

"Stop it," Echo directed firmly, but with love. "This is the best day of your life, you're about to marry by far the most eligible bachelor in the entire state of Louisiana, and you're going to live happily ever after," she met her best friend's eyes in the mirror. "You're nervous, you're shaky, and in about an hour, when it's all over and you're partying with the rest of us, you're going to be on cloud nine. Then you're going to be on the most fabulous honeymoon ever, and you'll forget all about whatever it is right now that's making you lose your mind," she assured the quivering bride.

"I know how to make you forget all about your nerves, even if it's only for a moment," Cheryl smiled at her shyly in the mirror.

"Oh, thank goodness," Missy sighed. "Give it to me... what's your secret?" she demanded, desperate for something to take her mind off of her unfounded worries.

The young woman blushed and smiled an angelic smile.

"A baby?!" Missy clapped her hands together in hopeful delight, and when Cheryl nodded, turned to embrace her.

"It's early yet, so we're not telling everyone, but we knew that you would want to know," she beamed.

"Oh, honey, I'm so excited for you two!" the bride's eyes welled with tears, her jitters completely forgotten for the moment.

"Hey, hey! None of that!" Echo scolded, a bit misty herself. "You'll smear your makeup," she dabbed at her friend's eyes delicately with a tissue.

"Oh, goodness, you're right," Missy fanned her face, trying to stave off her happy tears.

"Told you I'd make you forget to be scared," Cheryl winked at her boss and received a grateful hug.

Missy looked from Cheryl to Echo and back again. "I don't know what I'd do without you two," she whispered, welling up again.

"You'll never have to know," Echo replied, pulling in the other two for a group hug.

Ben rapped softly on the door. "Ladies, it's time…" he called, waiting for them to let him in.

The man who had been like a son to Missy was admitted, looking slightly awkward but adorable in his tuxedo. His vest was a soft peach color, to match the bridesmaid's dresses, and his silk cravat looked like it might be choking him a bit, but the way his wife looked at him when he entered the room was a sight to behold. She kissed him on the cheek as she and Echo went downstairs to take their places.

"Hey, Papa Bear," she grinned. "Congratulations!"

"Thanks," Ben blushed, as his wife had, and gratefully accepted Missy's hug. "But she wasn't supposed to tell you until the reception, when we were all together," he protested.

"Desperate situations called for desperate measures, darlin'," his boss chuckled.

"You ready for this?" he asked, the love and concern for her evident in his eyes.

The bride-to-be nodded with serene confidence. Her girls had gotten her through the panic stage, and now she couldn't wait to walk down the petal strewn aisle through her decked out back yard and into the gazebo to marry the most wonderful man on the planet.

"Yes, I really am," she confessed with a starry-eyed smile. "Ben, come here for a second," she beckoned, holding out a hand to him that he took and knelt beside her where his darling wife had been moments before.

"You're like the son I never had," she told him, lightly touching his cheek. "I could not have made it this far without you, and I just want you to know how much I love you, and Cheryl and baby Cammie. Wherever you go, whatever you do, you can always count on the fact that you'll always be in my heart, and I'm only a phone call away if you ever need me," she stopped for a moment, fanning her face again, trying not to cry.

"I'm not gonna lie, darlin', it makes my heart hurt to think that I won't be seeing y'all every day," she admitted, her southern accent profound, in the emotion of the moment. "But I'm so happy that you're going to be spreading your wings and doing what you were meant to do," she nodded, her face radiating the love that she had for this very special young man.

Ben squeezed her hand, clearing his throat and looking down for a few seconds before returning his gaze to hers.

"I can't even begin to tell you how much you've meant to me, ever since we first met," he began, clearing his throat again. "My mother has been out of the picture for so long that I barely remember her, but you've been a mom to me the entire time I've known you, and..." he paused, swiping a hand briefly across his eyes and taking a deep breath before continuing. "...there are no words that could possibly express how thankful I am to have you in my life. You're always there for me. No matter what I do, I know that ultimately, everything will be okay because you've got my back. I have the courage to do whatever I need to do in life, because I know that you believe in me. I love you Ms. G., you're the best mom that a guy could ask for," he finished, his voice trembling with emotion as Missy pulled him into a hug, no longer caring that her mascara might smear.

After their moment, both of them pulled back and smiled, relieved that what they'd both felt for so long had finally been articulated. Ben pulled a tissue from the box on the vanity, muttering something about Echo hunting him down if Missy came downstairs with mascara on her face, and handed it to his boss, his mentor, his mom.

He stood, brushing any possibly wrinkles from his

tux, and offered his arm to the lovely woman in front of him. "Ready?" he asked. Standing slowly, she nodded and took his arm.

Missy's backyard and gazebo had been transformed into fairyland for the event, with white and silver streamers and bunting bedecking every surface, and so many floral arrangements that the yard smelled positively heavenly. The guests were seated in skirted white chairs on both sides of a white runner that had been strewn with white rose petals, and the entire effect was breathtaking and magical, but what made Missy inhale sharply as she entered the yard on Ben's arm, moving in time with the music, was the sight of her beloved Chas, looking positively stunning in his tuxedo. Every doubt she'd ever had washed away, and she couldn't wait to be Mrs. Gladstone-Beckett.

The wedding had been specifically tailored to the couple, so when Ben walked Missy down the aisle, he took his place beside Chas, as the best man. The other groomsman, Grayson, led Toffee and Bitsy on leashes down the aisle, with a ring box attached to each of the canine's collars, and stood beside Ben, with their furry friends sitting, waiting patiently, until the rings were needed. The ceremony was short, heartfelt and beautiful, with Chas and Missy speaking the vows that they had written for each other, which left the attendees in tears, and when he kissed her after being pronounced man and wife, she even didn't hear the cheers of friends and loved ones, she was so lost in the moment.

Missy and Chas's reception was held at the country club, and it seemed that all of LaChance and Dellville were in attendance. Chas had arranged for Becca Rogers, who was, hands down, the best clambake caterer on the east coast, to come all the way to Louisiana to handle the food for the reception. He and Missy flew to Cape Cranston to meet with the spunky and creative culinary genius, and the trio hit it off immediately. Missy had balked a bit initially at the expense of bringing in someone who wasn't local, but Chas was from New York originally and had heard nothing but rave reviews about Becca, so she had agreed to meet her. Once the two gals met, all doubts in Missy's mind were promptly erased.

She rationalized that more of Chas's wealthy family and friends from New York might attend if they at least knew that the reception fare would meet their standards.

The couple had a rare moment alone, after the formalities of dinner, cake-cutting, bouquet and garter tossing and dancing, where they stood, gazing out at the excitement and laughter of family and friends.

Chas turned to his bride and took her hands, looked into her eyes and opened his mouth to speak, when suddenly the boisterous drawl of none other than Mayor Felton Chadwick shattered their moment of solitude.

"Well, well, well, it's a fine day. A fine day indeed," Felton clapped Chas on the shoulder and gave a rather startled Missy a kiss on the cheek. The rotund man had outdone himself in dressing for the occasion, resplendent in a white walking suit with a light blue shirt and red and white tie, his bald pate gleaming. The mayor always seemed to prefer wearing some sort of red, white and blue whenever attending a function where many of his constituents might be about. He had been re-elected by a landslide, so one would think that his posture would be a bit more relaxed, but he worked the reception crowd like a pro, shaking hands and kissing babies with gleeful abandon.

"Yes, it is. Thank you for coming, Felton," Chas replied, shaking his hand and ignoring the raised eyebrows of his new wife.

"And my dear, you are just a picture of radiant loveliness," the mayor drawled, taking Missy's hand and kissing it.

"Thank you, Mayor Chadwick," she managed a polite smile.

"Well, I do believe I'm going to help myself to another piece of that delightful wedding cake, and leave you two lovebirds to get better acquainted," he winked slyly. "Congratulations y'all," he waved, heading for the dessert table.

"You invited the mayor?" Missy blinked at him.

"Sweetie, it was the right thing to do. We know what he's like, but we also know that he's not an enemy that a business owner wants to have in this small community," her husband reminded her gently.

She sighed, nodding. "You're right. I'm still just peeved."

"Let it go sweetie, we have more important things to think about," he grinned, waggling his eyebrows, and kissed her.

Chapter 15

"Did I show you where the dog treats are kept?" Missy asked Echo, going over her list of instructions with a fine-toothed comb. Echo's ice cream shop had sold just before the wedding, but she wasn't moving until after Missy and Chas came back from their honeymoon because she had agreed to watch the dogs while they were gone.

"Three times," Echo sighed, rolling her eyes melodramatically. "Seriously, dear, get yourself in the car and get out of here before your long-suffering husband loses his mind," she ordered, pushing her friend toward the door.

"But did you..." she began, as she was being herded out.

"Yes, I did! Whatever it is, yes. Get moving sister," Echo laughed at Missy's inordinate attention to detail when it came to taking care of her furry babies. "Yes, I have your phone number, and the number of the B&B, as well as the veterinarian's number. I love your girls as much as you do and I'll take good care of them," she reassured her, propelling her out the door, meeting the eyes of an amused and grateful Chas.

He'd had the car loaded and had been standing by it, waiting patiently, for nearly half an hour, while Missy went around making certain that all supplies were stocked, all of her instructions were understood, and that Echo had all of the resources that she could possibly need.

They were seated in the car and he started backing out of the driveway, with Echo waving from the porch, when Missy called out, "Wait!"

Stopping the car, Chas looked at her inquisitively. She pushed down the button to lower the window and called out to Echo. "When you take them to the park..."

"...be sure to take their water bowls, a Frisbee, and a

ball in the special backpack," her friend finished her sentence for her. "I know, I know, it's bullet point number fourteen," she called from the porch, opening the screen door to go inside before Missy could think of anything else.

"Thank you, love," Missy called out as the door closed behind her chuckling friend.

"Ready?" Chas asked.

"Ready," she nodded with a grin, finally able to stop worrying about the girls long enough to get excited about embarking upon her honeymoon.

The bed-and-breakfast that the happy couple had booked for their honeymoon was a gracious, antiqued-filled mini-mansion, nestled among palms and evergreens on a private stretch of pristine beach along the Florida coast.

"Oh, Chas, it's beautiful!" Missy exclaimed when they got out of their rental car, drinking in the ocean breeze. She couldn't wait to kick off her shoes and feel the sand between her toes.

"Not as beautiful as my lovely wife," he grinned, taking her hand and heading for the foyer.

A tall, thin woman with iron-grey hair was watering plants on the spacious front porch when they approached, and she put her watering can down, extending her hand.

"You must be Missy and Chas," her tone was warm. "I'm Maggie, your host, housekeeper, and concierge for the next week. Come on inside and I'll show you around," she invited, turning the ornate, egg-shaped doorknob to admit them.

The Beach House B & B managed to be exquisitely decorated and comfortable all at once, with plush Persian carpets underfoot, gleaming mahogany antiques throughout, and hand-tatted lace at the leaded-glass windows. The stately home had stood amongst the picturesque beauty since before the Civil War, and had been meticulously updated and maintained in period style. Stepping into the grand foyer, with crystal chandeliers above, was like stepping back in time, and Missy was spellbound.

Maggie showed them the elegant dining room where they'd be served breakfast with the other guests of the inn every morning, as well as the library, two parlors, the rec room, the courtyard, formal gardens, and pool area, before showing them upstairs to their suite. The burgundy floral interior of the Honeymoon Suite featured a king-sized, four-poster mahogany bed with sumptuous linens, an opulent living area, a sun porch, and a huge, white marble clad bathroom with a whirlpool tub that looked large enough to swim in. Leaving the newlyweds to explore their temporary home, Maggie let them know that there would be an afternoon tea service in the Wedgewood Parlor at 3:00 and invited them to come and enjoy refreshments and meet the other guests.

While Chas retrieved their luggage, Missy practically dove into the beach bag that she'd brought in with her, and changed into the sassy cerulean swimsuit that she'd purchased specifically for the honeymoon. Feeling slightly self-conscious, she was nonetheless determined to indulge in her share of fun in the sun. As soon as her husband, (getting accustomed to using that term in reference to the handsome detective was a slow process), returned with their things, he quickly donned his suit and, throwing a couple of towels into the top of their beach bag, they headed down the weathered grey boardwalk that led to the beach.

The Beach House had thoughtfully provided lounge chairs, sunbrellas, and foam floating rafts for the enjoyment of their guests. Setting up two loungers under a turquoise and green striped sunbrella that was several feet away from the nearest beachgoers, Missy and Chas strolled hand in hand down the sugar sand beach toward the azure waters of the Gulf. The water was cool and refreshing, and they swam and splashed and played like teenagers for nearly an hour, before heading back to their loungers to relax and dry in the warm Florida breeze. Toweling off, Missy noticed that a small cooler, with a note on top that said, "Compliments of the Beach House," had been left between their chairs. Spreading out her towel on the lounger and easing onto it, she slipped the lid off of the cooler and found that it had been stocked with ice-cold bottled water, coconut water, and mango juice.

Chas selected coconut water and Missy grabbed a mango juice to enjoy while they recovered from their swim.

"Mmmm...this feels so good," she smiled, reclining, eyes closed beneath her sunglasses.

"I could get used to this," Chas agreed, setting his coconut water in the cup holder that was molded into the side of his lounger.

Their tranquil afternoon was interrupted just then, by the sound of voices raised in anger. Missy and Chas glanced over to see what was causing the commotion, and witnessed what looked like a marital spat happening between a couple who had settled under a sunbrella that was nearly a football field away. There was a man and a woman, who looked to be in their 50's, clad in swimsuits, sitting in beach chairs, yelling at each other and making aggressive gestures. The newlyweds shared an uncomfortable look, then Chas shrugged and they both laid back and closed their eyes, trying their best to ignore the couple. They were far enough away that, despite their voices being heard, their words were unintelligible. Several minutes later, the wife stood up, hastily wrapped a large towel around her middle and tried to stalk away. Her husband grabbed her arm, and Chas was halfway out of his chair to intervene if necessary, when the man released his wife with a forceful shove and she ran, barefoot toward the inn.

"What should we do?" Missy asked, wide-eyed, her heart beating fast after having witnessed the awful event.

"Nothing...yet," Chas said, his jaw flexing.

The angry man flopped back down in his lounger, crossed his arms over his chest and seemed to go to sleep. The mood ruined, Missy and Chas waited long enough to make sure that the woman would have had adequate time to walk to the inn in privacy, then gathered their things and left quietly, choosing to lay by the pool to dry off. They took the cooler with them to the pool, which was mercifully deserted.

"Do you think she's okay?" Missy worried as they floated lazily in the shallow end.

The detective shrugged. "We can only hope so. People make strange choices sometimes." He glanced at his waterproof watch. "If we want to go to afternoon tea, we should probably head back to the room in half an hour."

"I think I'd like to give it a try. We don't have to attend every day, but it'd be nice to meet some of the other guests, don't you think?"

"Whatever you'd like, sweetie. I'm happy wherever I am, as long as I'm with you," Chas charmed her with a smile and a kiss, tasting the salt of the ocean on her lips.

"I hope the woman from the beach is okay," she went back to worrying, biting her lower lip.

"I hope so too, sweetie, but there's nothing we can do at this point, so you need to stop worrying about it and focus on enjoying your honeymoon," he directed.

"Sorry. I'll pay attention to us from now on," she promised, pulling herself up over the concrete edge of the pool and walking quickly to her sun chair.

"Good," her husband replied, following her lead.

Chas was fully dressed in white linen trousers and a camel-colored button-down, but Missy still had to dry her hair before tea, so she sent him down first, to scout out the situation and let her know what it was like. She dried her hair, picking up her phone when she saw the screen light up with a text from her husband.

"You're going to love this! Finger sandwiches, Petit Four cakes, English teas, all served on fine china...come on down when you're ready!"

Missy smiled, reaching for her can of hairspray, excited to experience tea time at the Beach House. The guest rooms in the mansion opened up to a common hall that went to the left and the right at the top of the grand staircase. She pulled the door shut behind her, twisting the knob to make certain that it was locked, and started for the stairs, almost crashing into someone coming out of the room next door.

"Oh, excuse me!" she smiled apologetically, finding herself face to face with the woman from the beach. Before she could think to stop herself, she glanced quickly down at the woman's arm, seeing the beginnings of a nasty bruise where she'd been manhandled.

"No problem," the woman smiled tightly, clearly annoyed.

Impulsively, Missy decided to reach out to the battered woman. "I'm sorry, I don't mean to pry, but..."

Before she could even attempt to finish her sentence, the faked smile disappeared from the woman's face. "Then don't!" she snapped. "I don't know who you think you are, little miss busybody, but you should just keep your nose in your own business if you know what's good for you," she snarled, turning her back on Missy and moving toward the stairs.

"I'm sorry, I..."

"Drop dead," the woman said, without bothering to turn around.

Missy felt the color rising in her cheeks as she waited a moment before taking the stairs down. She was just trying to be kind, there was really no reason for that woman to have been so rude. Remembering what Chas had said, she tried as best she could to shake it off, and made her way to the parlor, shocked when she saw the woman from the hall cuddled up to the man who had roughed her up on the beach.

She caught Chas's eye from across the room and glanced subtly at the couple. He inclined his head, indicating with a look, that she should just leave it alone, and she made her way over to him, snagging a delicate china cup of Earl Grey on her way.

"Try this," Chas popped a bite of finger sandwich into her mouth when she finally reached him.

"Oh, my goodness, that's delicious," she raved, holding her hand in front of her mouth to be polite. She swallowed, then took a sip of tea to wash down the bite. The newlyweds sampled more of the delicious tidbits that were staged on crystal dishes, fine china and silver platters, each bite more wonderful than the last, and circulated among the other twenty or so guests who were milling about, meeting warm and lively folks from all over the country who were vacationing at the inn. They made a point of avoiding the couple from the beach, but Missy accidentally bumped into the woman yet again when she went to the table to pluck another sweet shrimp from the silver shrimp tree.

"Do you ever watch where you're going?" she demanded shrilly.

"I'm sorry, I didn't mean to," Missy started to apologize, despite the woman's rudeness.

"Yeah, well, you see what happened the last time you "didn't mean to" run into me," she snipped, indicating the bruise on her arm.

"That's a lie!" Missy exclaimed, a little too loudly, drawing puzzled looks from the other guests. "That happened to you on the beach, I saw him," she pointed to the man who was standing behind the woman, "grab you and push you. You know darn well that I didn't do that!" her kitten grey eyes flashed fire.

The woman's eyes narrowed and just as she opened her mouth to respond, Chas intervened smoothly.

"Excuse me ma'am," he spoke to the woman in a low, cordial voice. "I'm going to have to steal this lovely lady away from you for a moment, won't you excuse us?" he smiled politely, spiriting Missy away before her temper burst forth again.

"Good riddance," Missy heard as they glided to the far side of the parlor where they could have a bit of privacy.

"Chas, that, that...woman..." she began.

"Is entirely wrong and we both know it," he said gently. "I vote that we go back upstairs, get dressed up and head into town for a really expensive dinner, what do you say?" he suggested, trying to distract his fuming bride. Not trusting herself to speak, she shot a dark glance at the woman's back and nodded. They took a wrong turn down one of the corridors downstairs, trying to find the back staircase to their room, and happened to end up near the administrative office, where they heard the sound of someone crying. Peeking in the door, Missy saw their host, sitting at her desk, wiping away tears and trying to pull herself together enough to return to the tea party.

"Maggie?" she knocked softly on the door frame, startling the poor woman. "Are you okay? Is there anything we can do?" she asked, moving slowly into the office with Chas behind her.

The innkeeper smiled wanly, wiping her face with a tissue. "I'll be okay, I just spoke with the owner of the inn, and he said that he has to sell it. His wife has been in poor health for quite some time, and they just don't want the hassle of dealing with yet another business," she explained.

"Oh, no! That's awful," Missy sympathized.

"Yes, it is," Maggie nodded. "This place has been a respite for travelers for more than a hundred years, and when it closes, not only is it the end of an era, but it'll be the end of my job," her lower lip trembled, and she bit down to still it.

"What if someone new bought it? Could it stay open then?" she asked, trying to give her hostess some hope.

"Even if they did, there's no guarantee that they'd keep it as a B & B, or that they'd retain me. Developers have been trying to get at this prime piece of real estate for years," Maggie sighed. "I'm sorry, I probably shouldn't even be talking to you about this," she shrugged hopelessly.

"Don't feel bad," Missy replied. "We won't say anything. If we can help in any way at all while we're here, just let us know, okay?" she offered, her southern hospitality rising to the surface.

"Thanks, but I'll manage," Maggie attempted a smile. "You two enjoy your evening."

Chas drove them into the nearest town and headed for a 5-star seafood restaurant that he'd read about before making the trip to Florida. Since it was a weekday, and they arrived just after five o'clock, getting in wasn't a problem, and sooner than they expected, they were making goo-goo eyes at each other across the table, and enjoying an ocean view and sunset that was spectacular. They had an amazing meal which included sweet, tender lobster tails, a chunky, creamy clam chowder, and young, succulent asparagus. The cuisine reminded Missy of the delightful fare that Becca Rogers had created for their wedding reception, and the memory brought a smile to her face.

"What?" Chas asked, taking her hand across the table and enjoying her contented expression.

"I'm just so happy," she confessed, twining her fingers in his. "You know, I've been thinking..." she began.

"Uh-oh, that means trouble," her husband teased.

She grinned and squeezed his hand. "I've been thinking," she continued, "...that with Ben and Cheryl moving away, Echo moving away, and everything else that's happened in LaChance the last couple of years...maybe it's time for a change," she shrugged.

"A change? What kind of change?" Chas asked, his blue eyes dazzling her.

"Like, maybe we should move..." she trailed off, looking at him hopefully.

"I'm not opposed to the idea," he answered agreeably. "What did you have in mind?" Chas's options were wide open. Because of his huge inheritance, he could live anywhere he wanted to, and now that they were married, the same applied to Missy.

"Well, when Maggie said that the owner of The Beach House was selling it, it gave me an idea. I've always thought that it would be fun to own a bed-and-breakfast, and if we bought that one, we could keep it open, Maggie could keep her job, the developers wouldn't be able to swoop in and bulldoze it, and I could have a cupcake bakery down here," she enthused.

"So, you've already plotted out a course to save the world, haven't you, my tender-hearted wife?" Chas asked, loving her more every minute.

"And the dogs would love the beach and the ocean, and we could go for long walks and swim whenever we wanted…" she continued her previous thought.

"But what about my work? I wouldn't think there'd be much for a detective to do in this sleepy little area," he pointed out.

"Oh. I hadn't really thought about that part of it. Do you have to do police work? Couldn't you just take people out cruising in a sailboat or something?"

Chas took a breath, thinking for a moment before responding. "Sweetie, I have to have a purpose in life. If I'm not working at doing something that helps people, I'm going to feel useless," he explained.

Missy nodded, filled with admiration for the man she married. "I understand. What about charity work? Would that make you feel good?"

"I do charity work along with my job," he reminded

her. Seeing her deflate a bit, he changed tactics. "Let's head back to the inn and do more talking," he suggested. "I like the idea, we just need to think things through a bit. I just don't know that there'd even be enough police work down here to keep me busy."

He paid the check and they were mostly quiet, just enjoying each other's company, on the way home. Missy yawned repeatedly, and looked forward to climbing into their massive feather bed.

They walked into the front foyer and were startled by a bloodcurdling scream. Maggie dashed inside, wild-eyed. "There's a body in the pool!"

Chas and Missy looked at each other, Missy was scared, Chas was resolute. "Maybe there's a purpose for me here after all," he said grimly, heading for the pool area.

Did you enjoy this story? Check out book 16 in the series today!

Chocolate Filled Murder

> Special Pomegranate Pleaser Cupcakes

Cupcakes

1 - 16 oz bottle of pomegranate juice

2 eggs at room temperature

1/4 stick unsalted butter, at room temperature

1 1/3 cups sugar

¼ cup vanilla yogurt

1 ½ tsp baking powder

1/4 tsp baking soda

1 1/2 cups All-Purpose flour

Special Pomegranate Pleaser Cupcakes

Reduce 16 oz. pomegranate juice to ¾ cup.

Cream together butter and sugar.

Beat in eggs, one at a time until pale yellow in color.

Add add yogurt and pomegranate juice.

Sift together baking powder, baking soda and flour.

Add dry ingredients to the wet ingredients. Stir until incorporated.

Preheat oven to 350 degrees.

Pour batter to fill 2/3 of cupcake liner.

Bake cupcakes for 15-17 minutes and check with a toothpick.

If the batter does not stick to toothpick, then the cupcakes are done.

Makes 18-24 cupcakes.

Vanilla Buttercream Frosting

¼ stick (2 Tbsp) unsalted butter, at room temperature

2 cups powdered sugar

Special Pomegranate Pleaser Cupcakes

1 tsp pure vanilla extract

1/4 cup heavy whipping cream

2 Tbsp sour cream

Beat butter, sour cream and vanilla extract together.

Add heavy whipping cream and powdered sugar, alternating between the two until you get the consistency you desire.

Pipe onto cooled cupcake.

About the Author

Summer Prescott is a USA Today and Wall Street Journal Best-Selling Author, who has penned nearly one hundred Cozy Mysteries, and one rather successful Thriller, The Quiet Type, which debuted in the top 50 of its genre. As owner of Summer Prescott Books Publishing, Summer is responsible for a combined catalog of over two hundred Cozy Mysteries and Thrillers. Mentoring and helping new Cozy writers launch their careers has long been a passion of Summer's, and she has played a key role in the incredible success of Cozy writers such as Patti Benning and Carolyn Q. Hunter.

Summer enjoys travel, and is honored to be a featured speaker at the International Writer's Conference in Cuenca, Ecuador, in May 2018. The event draws writers from all over the world.

In an exciting development, Summer has recently been asked to write monthly for her favorite magazine, Atomic Ranch. Having been an Interior Decorator before giving up her business to write full-time, Summer is thrilled by the opportunity and looking forward to having her writing published in the only magazine to which she actually subscribes.

Summer is a doting mother to four grown children, and lives in Champaign, Illinois with her Standard Poodle, Elvis.

Author's Note

I'd love to hear your thoughts on my books, the storylines, and anything else that you'd like to comment on—reader feedback is very important to me. My contact information, along with some other helpful links, is listed on the next page. If you'd like to be on my list of "folks to contact" with updates, release and sales notifications, etc.... just shoot me an email and let me know. Thanks for reading!

Also...

... if you're looking for more great reads, Summer Prescott Books publishes several popular series by outstanding Cozy Mystery authors.

Contact Summer Prescott

Website http://summerprescottbooks.com

Email: summer.prescott.cozies@gmail.com

Newsletter: Sign Up

And...be sure to check out the Summer Prescott Cozy Mysteries fan page and Summer Prescott Books Publishing Page on Facebook – let's be friends!

Made in United States
Orlando, FL
13 March 2022